My Corfu Love Story

A clean romance novella

by

Effrosyni Moschoudi

© *2022 Effrosyni Moschoudi. All rights reserved.*

Effrosyni Moschoudi asserts the moral right to be identified as the author of this work.

Cover design: © 2022 Melinda De Ross. All rights reserved.

This book is licensed for the personal enjoyment of the original purchaser only. This book may not be resold or given away to other people. If you would like to share this book with another person, please purchase an additional copy for each recipient. If you are reading this book and did not purchase it, or if it was not granted to you directly by the author for your use only, then please purchase your own copy. Thank you for respecting the hard work of this author.

This is a work of fiction. Names, characters, places, and incidents either are the products of the author's imagination or are used fictitiously, and any resemblance to locales, events, business establishments, or actual persons - living or dead - is entirely coincidental.

Effrosyni Moschoudi

For my grandmother Antigoni, and all grandmothers in Heaven

Contents

Chapter 1 5
Chapter 2 8
Chapter 3 11
Chapter 4 13
Chapter 5 15
Chapter 6 21
Chapter 7 26
Chapter 8 30
Chapter 9 36
Chapter 10 39
Chapter 11 43
Chapter 12 49
Chapter 13 54
A NOTE FROM THE AUTHOR 61
MORE FROM EFFROSYNI 62
ABOUT THE AUTHOR 65

Chapter 1

Spyri woke up to the sound of cicadas. For her, it was the sweetest sound in the world. It signalled that she was back in Greece, back in her beloved village of Moraitika in Corfu, the most precious place in the world to her.

Here, she'd spent countless long summers with her grandparents, her father's parents, away from the mad bustle of London where she grew up, the daughter of a Greek man and an English woman.

Nowadays, being a thirty-three-year-old restaurant owner in London, Spyri no longer had the luxury of long holidays abroad, but going to Corfu for a fortnight every summer was something she'd never give up. Moraitika, to her, was as precious as oxygen.

And here she was again, on the first morning of her holiday in Granny's house. This is how she'd come to think of the house now, since her grandfather had passed away many years earlier.

My first day in Corfu! The thought made Spyri jump out of bed as if it was on fire. She drew the curtains and looked outside the bedroom window. The garden of the house next door was in bloom, sweet basil and rosemary wafting in the breeze, and she drew a deep breath with half-closed eyes as the gentle morning sunlight caressed her face.

Spyri went downstairs and made a beeline for the kitchen. She put water in the kettle and opened the cupboard hoping to find some tea bags. Her grandmother materialized beside her, as if conjured up from thin air, all frail and tiny, just as Spyri took a glass jar into her hands and grimaced.

The old woman chuckled to see her sour expression. Spyri had never cared for the dried herb stored in that old jar.

"Oh, Granny! All these years you never drank any other tea than *tsai tou vounou*! Why are the people here so hung up on mountain tea? It's beyond me. I mean, you can't even have it with milk! I must remember to visit the supermarket today and get some *English Breakfast*. Now, where's the coffee?" She began to rummage through the cupboard, moving jars and mugs around, to try to find it. She was sure she'd left a new jar of instant coffee granules in there last summer.

"Come on, never mind all that, *Spyri mou*! Tell me your news. Last night when you came we had no time to talk. When are you bringing a man with you? You always come on your own!" the old woman said with a benevolent smile as she took her time to sit at the table. Her arthritic legs and back gave her hell throughout the year. This was why she moved cautiously, having suffered too many nasty falls.

Spyri stole glances at her, the sight endearing. She'd just found the coffee and was now trying to open another old jar, the one for the sugar this time. Finally, she gave up with a grunt. "Why do you insist on using these jars? Rust and humidity have sealed them all shut. Where are the ones I brought you last summer?"

Her grandmother gave a familiar knowing smile that signalled the answer to Spyri in an instant.

"You gave them away to one of the neighbours, didn't you? Oh, Granny, why did you do that? I brought them for *you*! Not Marianna or Kaliopi, or Mrs Eleni from Albania..."

The old woman waved her hand dismissively. "They needed them more than I did. They're poor people, *agape mou*. Besides, I'm happy with my old jars. I've had them all my life. They are the ones I used to make your grandad's tea and your own milk and cocoa drinks when you were little, remember?"

Spyri walked up to where her grandmother sat, squeezing her shoulder fondly, her eyes misting over. Old memories from her precious childhood summers with her grandparents in this house, this heavenly village and island, had the knack of stirring her heart to form an unbearable mix of deep heartache and longing. To shake it off, she had another attempt at opening the sugar jar in her hands, and managed it this time, causing her grandmother to giggle.

"See? There's nothing to it. If I can open them with my gnarly old hands, then so can you." Granny winked playfully. "And now, out with it. Don't change the subject! When are you going to find a man and settle down? I'm an old woman, you know. I don't have long to go!"

Chapter 2

After a quick breakfast, Spyri took the downhill path to the beach for her first swim, her flower-patterned dress billowing softly around her legs, her wood-soled sandals clip-clopping on the concrete path.

As she strode along, she raised her hand every now and then to greet the locals. Some were milling about in their gardens or sitting outside their front doors having a snack at plastic garden tables. Others greeted her from shop fronts, or rode by in their mopeds.

By the time she'd arrived at the beach she'd exchanged greetings and pleasantries with at least a dozen people. It always happened that way. And she knew, without a single doubt, that this afternoon when she'd have a walk down the main road, the rest of her acquaintances and extended family members would already have been informed she'd arrived. Moraitika was a small place and news of who was returning for their annual summer holiday travelled really fast.

She found her usual spot under a tree by the jetty and laid out her beach mat. As she took off her dress, admiring her new bright-coloured tankini, her mind began to wonder. Old memories flooded her mind about people she once knew, who used to swim here with her over the years.

She also recalled the trouble she used to have with the locals back in the day. Village gossip was a huge problem for her. Meeting boys secretly would have been impossible, and she never attempted to do it. Neither her grandparents nor her father had been happy with Spyri having much to do with young lads, be it tourists or the village boys. Spyri had always been a good girl, and so had decided to stay away from boys to keep everyone happy.

Only once had her decision presented a problem. It was the unforgettable thirteenth summer of her life, when Markos from Salonica had come to visit his aunt Alexandra in the village. Back then, all the children would gather outside

Spyri's grandparents' house to sit at the front steps in the shade of a huge mulberry tree. In the early morning, and in the late afternoon, the village children would gather there to play cards, chat, joke around, and generally pass the time.

Spyri's family were happy for her to socialize with the village boys back then, mainly because she was in the presence of a multitude of cousins and not alone with anyone in particular.

That summer had been one to remember because of Markos. He had turned up one day with his cousins, and just like that, Spyri had fallen in love. She still recalled vividly his sweet smile, and those cypress-green eyes that were specked with gold and hardly ever looked straight at her. It was painful how shy he was!

She could hardly get a word out of him and, unlike the other boys, he never attempted to flirt with her. But she only had eyes for him. At midday, he would arrive at the beach, at this very spot where she had just laid out her things, to swim with his aunts and cousins just as she swam with her own family.

Day in and day out they would swim together with the other kids, then all of them would meet again in the evening back at the house. And they would chat and play there together every evening till the sun descended in the distant blue horizon, cooling the air delightfully, and colouring the step where they sat with a glorious golden hue.

During one of those evenings, Spyri was feeling exhausted as, that morning, her parents had rented a pedalo. Sitting next to Markos as one of the children shared a long-winded joke, without thinking, Spyri had leaned towards Markos and, ever so softly, put her head on his shoulder.

When she realized what she'd done she panicked, but then something occurred to her: that he hadn't moved away or complained. Instead, he'd tilted his head too, resting it against hers, and emitted a faint sigh that filled her heart with liquid heat. It felt like an explosion at first, rendering her dazed, then it dripped down to her stomach deliciously. She never forgot that feeling and hadn't experienced it again ever since.

Since that day, she'd known she was irrevocably in love with him. She'd told her female cousins about her feelings back then, and they tried to convince her to confess her love to him. When she insisted this was out of the question, they started to urge her to give him her address, so he could write to her from Salonica in the winter. The thought had kept her awake for a few nights as the last day of her holiday drew near. But even then, after all that contemplating, her shyness had won, and she never dared ask him if they could be pen pals.

That summer, it all ended between them on her last day with a simple goodbye in the late afternoon, then Markos took the path to his aunt's house with the other village boys. He gave her one last wave from a distance and that was it.

She never saw him again. His aunt would share snippets of news about him from time to time, as she and Spyri's grandmother were friends and often caught up on everyone's news during their chats.

Every year, Spyri would return to the village hoping to see Markos again but he never came. Instead, she'd hear all about his studies in Salonica, then about his fiancé, the woman he wound up marrying. In time, Spyri had given up on her hopes to see him again but, somehow, she never forgot him.

Markos was in her thoughts again now, as she slowly entered the water, stepping on smooth sand that glinted golden in the sunlight. The sea sparkled like a temptress dressed in her finest silk and jewels. The allure of the sea was so great in those moments that by the time she'd cooled enough to plunge into the water, her heart bursting with bliss, she had forgotten all about Markos again. For now.

Chapter 3

On her way home, Spyri greeted even more locals, and one of them imparted some sad news. Spyri was still deep in thought as she set the table. The meal was going to be basic today. These days, she could no longer count on her frail old grandmother to provide those unforgettable culinary triumphs of hers.

And so, Spyri was going to do all the cooking on this holiday and all the ones after that. This morning she'd had no time to cook, so she bought a few eggs, butter, bread, ham, and a can of *dolmades* from the mini market on the way home, then rustled up a quick lunch.

As she set the table, her mind was whirling still.

"What's wrong, *kyra mou*?" piped up her grandmother. Spyri could never fool her. She had no choice than to tell her what bothered her.

"Mrs Alexandra died yesterday. Did you know? I just heard."

The old woman heaved a huge sigh. "Of course. But why do you seem so upset? Alexandra lived her life... and she was well into her 90s."

"I know, but still..."

The old woman waved dismissively and gestured Spyri with a beaming smile to sit and eat, the way she always used to at mealtimes. "It's a one-way street for all the oldies in the village. We'll all go before you know it. The village is half-deserted as it is."

Spyri sat and picked up her fork. "I know... But it's so sad. The village keeps changing so fast. So many of the lovely people I knew are gone. So many houses that used to be full of life, their doors wide open, now stand deserted, derelict... Every year I come here, I find fewer and fewer of the kind, elderly people that I knew once... sometimes, I think I cannot stand it, you know? It breaks my heart." Spyri's eyes misted over.

Her grandmother raised a brow. "All that is understandable, *psyche mou*, but in Alexandra's case, are you sure your heartache is not a little about something else, too? Like, her nephew, Markos, maybe?"

Spyri was about to pop a forkful of omelette into her mouth, and the hand that held the fork froze, hovering in the air, as her mouth remained open for a few moments. Finally, she put the fork down, her lips twisting.

"Well, am I wrong or am I right?" the old woman pressed.

Spyri registered her knowing smile and knew then she had known all along about her feelings for Markos.

"You're wondering if Alexandra's passing might bring Markos back to the village, aren't you, *Spyri mou*?"

Spyri looked down at her full plate, and muttered, "Do you think he will come for the funeral, Granny? Has anyone said anything?"

Her grandmother's voice echoed bitter in her ears. "What do I know? I hardly ever leave this house any more." She patted her arthritic knees and added, "And hardly anyone visits me these days either. Who wants to enter a damp old house to shoot the breeze with a wrinkly like me?"

Spyri's heart melted. She knew her grandmother had been suffering with terrible loneliness over the past seven years since Grandad's death. "*I* do, Granny! *I* want to shoot the breeze with you!" She reached out and patted her hand.

The old woman squeezed Spyri's fingertips with her own gently, her eyes meeting hers.

Spyri saw a deep love in them that she knew would never die. No matter what.

The old woman chuckled and leaned back in her chair. "Now, eat up! And don't worry so much about it. If he's coming we'll soon find out."

Chapter 4

After an afternoon siesta Spyri got dressed to have a walk. She put on a white summer dress and slip on sandals, the kind of shoes that she could easily remove. She intended to walk along the beach after her long stroll down the main road. At the seafront, she loved to walk barefoot.

With a deep sigh, Spyri opened her jewellery box to find something to jazz up her look and to cheer herself up. As much as she loved this house, these days it filled her with so much sorrow, because of all the things she missed so much about the past, the things that time, ruthlessly, had forever stolen from her.

Both her beloved parents included, who had died just a couple of years apart. First, her mother from cancer, then her father from a broken heart. He had passed away last year and it had felt, oddly, like her losing her mother all over again too.

Spyri gave a forlorn sigh. All her life, she had enjoyed being an only child. Nowadays, she often wished she had a sibling, a sister perhaps...

But Spyri wasn't one to dwell in the past, allowing herself to wallow in self-pity. No, she knew better than that. This is why she shook her head, refusing to go there, to what she called Pity-Party-Town every time the sting of past hurts pricked her insides.

Instead, Spyri forced a smile to herself as she held in her hands a stunning jewellery set that consisted of a necklace, bracelet and earrings. They were made of silver, and blue Murano crystal – a beautiful souvenir she had bought for herself during a trip to Italy many years ago. The shade of the blue crystal matched her eyes.

Standing in front of the mirror, pleased with the result after putting the jewellery on, she used a fine brush on her long hair that fell on her shoulders in silky curls. Rummaging through the contents of a drawing cabinet, she soon found what she was after. It was one of the old ribbons from her teenage years

– her grandmother had kept so much from her old summers in there – and used it to tie a portion of her hair from the temples up.

The ribbon was fairly long. It held her hair loosely on the top of her head and snaked down the back almost to the edges of her locks. At its two ends, two tiny pink plastic baubles made delightful clicking sounds as they bumped against each other when Spyri looked around to make sure she'd left the room tidy.

Spyri entered the tiny living room, and her grandmother looked up from her knitting, her eyes looking huge behind her thick glasses. "Oh, Spyri, you dressed up for your walk! You look lovely!"

Spyri snorted with laughter remembering how her grandmother used to coax her into choosing more womanly attire to go on her evening walks as opposed to the casual shorts and t-shirts she'd spend all her mornings in. "Thanks, Granny. I knew it would please you."

The old woman winked. "Why don't you call at Mrs Alexandra's house on your way down to the main road? See if anyone's in? The funeral's tomorrow. You never know. He might be here."

Spyri sat beside her gran on the couch. "How did you guess? That's what I want to know."

"What? That you have an affinity for Markos?" She gave a playful huff. "Give me some credit, please! You were so transparent that summer! Alexandra and I were forever chuckling to watch you two. Why do you think I kept asking for his news over the years? I knew you had him in your heart." Granny's expression turned serious. "Spyri, I know you have him in your heart still. And something tells me you are in his too. It's worth going over there to see if he's in." She winked. "Just in case. But do it now. Today. I have a feeling. Humour me."

Chapter 5

Mrs Alexandra's house was in an elevated position compared to the road. Spyri felt stupid as she climbed the steps that led up to the garden gate. What was she doing? What was she hoping for? The man was married, for goodness sake. And chances were he wouldn't even remember her after all these years. Besides, Mrs Alexandra's house was a typical humble village home... Even if Markos had come to the island for the funeral, he'd probably never choose to stay in a place as basic as this.

Yet, as stupid as she felt, her urge to try her luck was stronger than ever today. None of her doubts was going to make her turn around. No way. And if he was here with his wife, it wouldn't be awkward. She'd only be visiting a childhood friend to say hi and offer her condolences.

Spyri tried the garden gate and saw it wasn't locked. She pushed it open and paced the short distance to the front door. Typically for a village house, it didn't have a doorbell. Normally, she would shout out the name of the occupant and they'd come out. Seeing that she couldn't tell with certainty who might be in, she raised a fist and gave the paint-chipped wooden door a gentle knock.

Moments later, she heard heavy footsteps from the inside of the house. When the door opened, her face bloomed like a flower. Before her, stood a heartthrob that she easily recognized as Markos. He was tall, much taller than she'd imagined he'd ever grow to be, and big, the kind of big in a man that makes you swoon. And swoon she did, as soon as his green eyes, those unforgettable emeralds, locked with hers, leaving her breathless.

"Spyri? Is that you?" he said, his jaw dropping.

He had just eyed her up and down, she saw that, but the sight of him had rendered her mesmerised other than that, her mind numb, and she couldn't tell if he was scoping her with admiration or just to make sure it was her.

"Yes... it's me..." she managed to say after a few moments. She ran an impatient hand through her hair and shifted her weight from foot to foot for a moment or two. "So pleased to see you, Markos. Welcome back... it's been a while."

"Yes, it has. Hasn't it?" He brushed his forehead with his fingertips and beckoned frantically to her to come inside. "Sorry for keeping you at the door just then. Please come in, I wasn't thinking. I arrived in the early hours of the morning and haven't slept at all... I'm beat," he said as they sat at a respectful distance from each other on an old worn-out couch.

"You've come for your aunt's funeral, I expect?" Only after she'd said it she realized her question was stupid.

"Yes, that's right..."

She swallowed hard, hoping to remove the huge knot lodged in her throat. "I am so sorry for your loss."

"Thank you, Spyri." He pinned his eyes on her, and the effect made her dizzy. In her mind, she was now counting the summers she'd spent here without seeing these eyes that she loved so much. Forever and a day had been lost.

As if guessing her thoughts he spoke then, his head tilted, a bright smile on his face. "How long has it been, Spyri? Twenty years?"

Spyri nodded mutely, her lips pressed together, her mind in a whirl. He'd said her name again and, just like earlier, it had sounded like sweet angel music in her ears. *Do I see a twinkle in his eyes every time he says my name?* His look was intense, like a beacon that was emitting a secret signal, a concealed message she was supposed to get.

But these were crazy thoughts. Surely, he was just saying her name and nothing else. She was only imagining these things. Goodness knows, over the years she'd been doing a lot of imagining, a lot of daydreaming about him. Somehow, no other man had ever meant to her anywhere near as much as he did. She'd had no steady relationships, and had barely had any romantic feelings for another man all this time. And then it hit her.

Is this why I've been shying away from men all my life? Have I been waiting for him to come back? Oh god! What now? While Spyri battled with inner thoughts and revelations, Markos had been eyeing her with a hint of uncertainty. Finally, he spoke up.

"I'd love to offer you tea or coffee, but I haven't had a good look around the kitchen yet, and I've no idea where to find things. Heck, I don't even know if my auntie owned a kettle!" He gave a cute smile and sprang upright, a single finger pointing to the back of the house.

"Do you want to come with me and have a look? I'm sure a woman will be more capable than me of finding their way around a kitchen. I'm useless with these things – a typical Greek male!" He laughed, a deep guttural sound that made her knees buckle.

Spyri gave a titter and rose from the couch. Just as he beckoned her to follow, she caught sight of his arms, rounded shoulders and strong torso under his close-fitting white shirt and felt a surge of desire to hold him overcome her. She saw herself in his arms then, as if in a dream, snuggling close against his chest, face buried in his neck, kissing it softly. One of her hands flew up, seemingly of its own accord, and she began to fan her face.

None the wiser, Markos opened the glass pane of the living room window a little wider on their way to the kitchen. "I know! Awfully hot again today! I bet it's much cooler in London! That's where you're staying still, right?"

Spyri smiled faintly and nodded as they entered Mrs Alexandra's kitchen. It looked as old as her grandmother's. Her eyes darted to the counter where two tattered glass jars stood, the wire around their necks rusty from the passing of time. *Identical to Granny's... Do they all shop from the same store here?* Entertained by her thoughts, she gave a little smile. She could see coffee and sugar inside the jars and guessed the contents would be rock-hard in this humid weather. She held up one of the jars to inspect it closely. She was right. Despite herself, she shook her head, lips pressed together. She could do without coffee.

Markos met her eyes and chortled. He held up a finger, turned on his heels and opened the fridge. "Aha! There's orange juice. The carton's unopened. Sell-by-date's fine. Would you like some?"

Five minutes later, they were sitting on the couch again, reminiscing about old times. Markos explained that his aunt, having had no children of her own, had left the house to him in her will. Her two nephews still resided in the village, her older sister's children, but seeing that they had a house and land on the island already, it had made sense to her to leave the house to Markos, her younger sister's child, who had no property there.

"My auntie knew how much I loved Moraitika. I've only spent one summer here my whole life, but I never..." He paused to clear his throat and looked away for a few moments, before turning to her again. "Well, I never forgot... the place. It's so beautiful. And now, I can make a home for myself here. The timing is incredible. I keep thinking it was meant to be. Bless her soul, my aunt was an angel. She treated me like a mother during the summer that I spent here. She never visited us in Salonica, but I never forgot her. I never forgot *anything* from that summer." His eyes penetrated hers more deeply. "You remember how lovely that summer was, don't you, Spyri?"

"Yes. Yes, of course I do, Markos." She looked away, pretending to admire an old frame that displayed a piece of embroidery. It depicted a basket of flowers on a table beside a cup and a teapot. And even though the colours had faded over time, Spyri could tell that when it was new, the picture must have been full of vibrancy, every flower a different, striking colour, the stems and leaves bright green, just like his eyes that, on the contrary, had remained just as bright as she remembered.

Suddenly, a thought ignited in her mind, stirring her curiosity. "What did you mean just now when you said you're going to make a home for yourself here? I thought your life is in Salonica?" She took a sip from her glass, trying to fake nonchalance, hoping she hadn't sounded as if she were complaining to him for never coming back.

To her surprise, when she drank and looked his way again, she saw his expression had changed to one of sorrow, almost regret. His head was bent down, eyes trained on the cotton rug under their feet.

"You know…" he finally said with a sigh. "My whole life has recently gone south, in a big way… My wife of ten years ran away with one of my closest associates a few months back. I'd like to say he used to be a friend, too, but I guess, he never really was." He scoffed and added, "You know… that man was as ugly as he was overweight, and a notorious womanizer. Never thought a woman could ever leave her husband to be with him. Let alone mine. Go figure…"

"Oh, Markos! This is terrible… I am so sorry…" she said feebly, clasping her hands together. It was all she could do to stop herself from flailing out her arms to draw him into a tight embrace. Her nails dug into her flesh causing her to wince. Luckily, he couldn't see. Lost in his thoughts, he kept his head bent.

He gave a wry little smile, his eyes turning to her for only a brief moment, then darting to the rug again. "Anyway, the divorce has been issued now. She got the house. I got my dignity back. I decided to leave the city and never return. My aunt's choice to leave me her house, coming at the right time, made my decision so much easier to make."

"I'm so sorry your marriage ended in that awful manner. I had no idea—"

"Don't be," he cut her off. "How would you know? I disappeared, didn't I?" He drank from his glass, emptying it. The tone in his voice made Spyri wonder. *Is he blaming himself?*

"Life happens to all of us, Markos… And I'm sure you had better things to do than come back to mucky Corfu for your holidays!" she joked and it worked. It elicited a loud chuckle from him and a half-smile.

To her surprise, he turned to her then, leaning forward, tilted his head and said, "It's getting awfully warm in here, Spyri. Fancy a walk? Down the beach where we used to swim back in the day? I bet you I can find the way there with my eyes shut!"

Chapter 6

Spyri and Markos walked side by side on their way to the beach, shooting the breeze and reminiscing, their eyes bright with mirth as they recalled memories from the summer they'd spent together as youngsters.

When they arrived at the beach, Markos walked up to the water. The tiny waves that came to lap gently on the shore splashed the front of his loafers, but he didn't seem to mind. He had his eyes closed now, arms spread wide apart, as he took in a deep breath, his head tilted back.

"Oh! How I've missed this beach, this place!" he said with a heavy sigh. When he turned to face Spyri, his expression was coloured with regret.

She knew instantly how he felt, even though he had said nothing else, and wondered if his regret could have anything to do with her at all, or if he was just feeling sorry that he had missed having so many magical summers here with his aunts and cousins.

She didn't have much time to ponder about it though because, out of the blue, he let out a cheer, and said:

"Look! The jetty! Do you remember, Spyri? We used to fish off its end! Can we go on it please?" He pointed to the sports jetty that stood at a close distance across from a hotel bar. The length of the beach from where they stood all the way to the jetty was lined with straw umbrellas. Bordering the lush lawn of the hotel property, a narrow wooden walkway ran the length of the beach as far as the eye could see.

"Of course," said Spyri with enthusiasm, even though she'd been on the jetty that morning. But she was happy to do whatever he wanted. Just being there with him felt like a surreal dream. "Can we use the walkway please?" She pointed to her sandals. "These aren't the best for walking on sand." Even though she'd normally grab a chance to walk on sand barefoot, she wanted badly to look pristine in his eyes.

Markos gave a cute little smile, looked down at his loafers, and shrugged his shoulders. "Sure. I'm easy either way." He didn't seem to mind they were wet at the toes. Smiling still, he gestured for her to go ahead.

As she walked along the walkway, Spyri could hear Markos's heavy footsteps behind her and still couldn't believe it was him following her. Everything had happened so quickly. Less than an hour ago, she was still unsure about visiting his aunt's house, and now she was on the beach, his intoxicating cologne wafting in the breeze, making her feel high. *High on love... And this doesn't even feel real... it'd better not be a dream or I'll wake up pretty cross in the morning!*

When they got onto the jetty, Markos approached her side again and, together, they walked to the end. There, they bent forward and looked down at the water in perfect sync, as if they had rehearsed it. The water was so serene and clear that they could see their faces on the surface, and every pebble on the seabed.

"Wow. All these years... where did they go?" he lamented out of the blue, turning to face her.

Spyri opened her mouth to say something jovial to change the mood. She could sense his sadness, and didn't understand it fully. She believed in moving forward, never lamenting, never regretting anything. She imagined he was upset over the divorce and the loss of his aunt. It would be best to change the subject. But, just then, noise from behind beat her to it.

There were a few people on the beach, guests at the hotel, no doubt, who sat at the bar. A little boy had been playing on the sand close by and was now shrieking at an ear-piercing volume. Another one stood before him, and they seemed to be fighting over a plastic little spade.

Neither of them seemed older than three or four years of age. A single bucket lay on the sand at their feet, and they both ignored it. The boys' chubby little hands were clutching the spade, both claiming it, like their lives depended on it. A man and a woman intervened to take the spade away and dissolve the tension between the kids. It had worked. A soothing silence ensued.

Markos turned away from the incident and shook his head as he focused his eyes on the deep blue sea in the shimmering distance. "Kids…" he lamented.

Spyri gave a frown. "What about them?"

"I'm glad I didn't have any."

Spyri tilted her head. "Oh? You and your wife didn't want any?" she blurted out before she could stop herself.

He turned to her, and she gazed into his face for a few moments. He looked tired, but not just because he hadn't slept, like he'd said earlier. And his eyes, they looked clear now, and more green than ever before. In her mind, he turned fifteen again, the boy who used to stand beside her on this very spot, teaching her how to fish with a line.

"No. Of course I wanted kids," he said finally. "A proper family! But my ex-wife didn't. I should have seen it coming, Spyri…" He shook his head again, his features hardening. "I had seen all the warning signs but chose to ignore them, to my detriment. She was a fair-weather friend. She wanted the good life, the fancy stuff, the big house… but not to run a house, not to have any responsibilities at all, let alone to raise any children."

He hung his head down, his gaze falling upon his loafers, long lashes shading his eyes, and Spyri couldn't see them any more. "It's still beyond me, how I could have been so blind for so long." His voice had grown frail, its volume reduced to almost a whisper by the end of his sentence.

A long sigh escaped from his lips, those lips Spyri had lost so much sleep over when she was a young girl. Now, a fully grown, independent woman, she'd have thought she'd be stronger. Yet, she felt the same urge again to kiss him the way she ached to do when they were young. And it took all her restraint not to put her arms around him.

Spyri's heart contracted with feeling to see him so upset, so full of bitterness. Instead of holding him, she allowed herself to put out a hand and squeeze his arm gently.

The gesture seemed to sober him up somewhat, and he looked up and away, eyes focusing far, at the distant shores of Epirus and Albania across the water.

"Don't get me wrong," he said after a while, avoiding her eyes. "I don't love her any more. Actually, I can't even recall what it was like to love her." He gave a tired smile. "The magnitude of her betrayal, and her nasty character as well, meant I found it easy to stop having any feelings for her. But I can't stop feeling sorry…"

Finally, he turned to look at Spyri and, impossibly, now took her hand in his. "I feel so sorry for the time I lost. For all the summers that I could have had here. With my lovely aunt, my beloved cousins and dear old friends… friends like *you*, Spyri."

The warm feeling of his hand in hers caused Spyri to gaze at him mutely, and a huge lump formed in her throat. Blinking profusely, she tried to process what he'd just said and done, and realized her heart was thumping against her chest. *What is he saying? Am I just a friend to him? And if he has been missing only a friend all this time why is he holding my hand? Is that a friendly gesture, or am I supposed to think there's more?*

Lost for words still, she looked down at their hands that were clasped together. His fingertips were caressing hers ever so softly. She felt delicious tingles in the pit of her stomach and wondered if old friends were allowed to do that and call it just friendship.

"Um… shall we keep walking? Would you like to sit and have a coffee somewhere?" she managed to say in the end, pointing at the far distance where a line of snack bars and small family hotels were built on the shore. She almost suggested they visit The Seashells, her favourite coffee bar, but thought better of it so he could pick the place instead.

His face went ablaze with excitement at the sound of her suggestion. "Yes! Can we go to The Seashells? For old times' sake! Remember my aunt and your grandmother used to take us there for ice cream? Please tell me it's still down there!"

To see the childlike enthusiasm on his face felt amazing. It transported her back to the old days. She gave a titter, feeling increasingly elated. He still held her hand, after all. "Yes, it's still there, Markos. Sadly, Mr Stathis has passed away. His children run it now. Come! I'll introduce you. Let's see if the oldest one still remembers you." She beckoned and they made their way to the base of the jetty, holding hands still, Spyri walking on air.

When they returned to the wooden walkway, Markos let go of her hand with an awkward smile and gestured to her to go on it first.

As they moved along to get to the bar, silently now, just one thought permeated Spyri's mind, torturing her... *Did he let go of my hand because we were going to go on the walkway again where it's impossible to walk side by side, or did holding my hand mean nothing? He probably feels upset and just needs a friend right now...*

Once again, Spyri scolded herself for thinking he might have romantic feelings for her after all this time. That is, if he ever had any to begin with.

Chapter 7

They had a chilled coffee at the bar, and a quick chat with the owners, none of which remembered Markos, as it turned out, much to his disappointment. But twenty years was a long time, and he remembered very little of them himself.

The two of them sat at a table on the sand and enjoyed their refreshing drinks. As they talked, Markos's mood lifted more and more.

Conversation flowed easily between them and, now, he was no longer talking about his losses but was full of questions about Spyri. After covering everything related to her work and previous studies, the travels she'd done, and her current likes and hobbies, inevitably, he asked if she was married. When she said she was single, he seemed incredulous. After that, he began to offer her one huge smile after another.

Hope rising inside her, Spyri's heart began to race every time he gazed into her eyes across the table. But her typical British reserve soon took over, and she never allowed herself to hope, let alone to flirt with him at all.

~~~

They had just left the bar, moving on along the shore. Markos had the idea to walk all the way to the neighbouring village of Messonghi. They could grab a bite to eat there at one of its cafés and restaurants by the river mouth. Going there along the beach entailed a ride in one of the tiny row boats that the local fishermen used to ferry visitors back and forth at the river mouth.

They ambled along, side by side, Spyri now barefoot on the sand and holding her sandals, since there was no walkway there. They were both cheering at the distant memory of that river crossing on the tiny boats, excited to know they'd soon be doing it again together after so long.

"It's the shortest ride ever, you must be joking, surely!" said Spyri, her expression bright. "I swear, it's just a mere pass from one side of the river mouth to the other. It lasts only seconds!"

Markos waved dismissively, screwing up his face. "No way! You're having me on. I remember it lasting for a good while!"

"What? You can't be serious!" She placed her hands, balled into fists, on her waist playfully. "I'll have you know that when the tide is out you can walk across the river mouth in just a few strides. I've done it, okay? You'll see when we get there!" she said with a giggle, quickening her pace, knowing that the look on his face would be priceless when he saw the crossing and realized that she was right. She found it hilarious to think that as a boy he had registered it in his memory like the most hazardous crossing ever, in a Great Rapids kind of way.

"Stop giggling, okay? I haven't had the benefit of going there year in and year out like you have, so there!" he teased, and when she met his eyes he winked, a wicked smile on his lips.

"Oh Markos, how I've missed you! We used to laugh so much, didn't we?" She'd blurted it out before she knew it, but she'd been lost in his smile, that smile that brought it all back, that made her daring, more so than she thought she had it in her to be.

To her surprise, he stopped short then and tilted his head. Then, he took two steps closer and stood before her at the edge of the shore, making her heart stop. He stood relaxed, arms at his sides, his delicious lips curling into a faint smile, the setting sun igniting the green of his eyes, making them look like two lush valleys set on fire. Inside her, a similar fire began to burn again.

"I've missed you too, Spyri... All this time, I never forgot you. Every summer, I... I kept wondering if you were holidaying here, if I'd ever see you again."

She swallowed hard, then said, "I've been thinking about you too, Markos. Wondering if you were ever coming back."

She managed to break their gaze and look away, turning around to admire the sunset.

The sun was almost touching the water now, and the surface of the sea seemed to boil with longing underneath the golden sphere of the heavens. Spyri could almost hear the sea sighing now, aching for its warm embrace with the sun that signalled the end of another day.

The same ache burned inside Spyri now, with Markos standing so close behind her. As she watched the breathtaking spectacle on the sky, making sounds about its beauty, she felt a rush of warm air on the back of her neck, the skin breaking into goosebumps.

For a crazy moment, she thought it was the rush of his breath, him coming up unbearably close behind her, but now she knew it had been the breeze that had burned hot on her skin, fooling her. She smiled to herself, feeling silly, and was about to turn around and prompt him to continue on their way, when she felt his touch.

Ever so gently, he had placed his hand on her shoulder. That, she knew with certainty, because he pulled her softly and turned her around.

Spyri faced him and saw tenderness in his eyes. The descending sun burned in them now, and it made his whole face glow. His skin had turned an orangey-golden hue. She looked down for a moment, dazed, to realize he had taken hold of her right hand in both of his.

"Spyri… tell me if I'm being too forward here, but…"

"Yes?" she asked in a mere whisper.

"I…" He looked away, only momentarily, then held her eyes again. "I never forgot you, Spyri… You know… I always thought of you, of that summer we spent together here, with the other kids. For me, you have always been…"

She saw it in his eyes then. And it was easy now. Now she knew with certainty what he was trying to say, and the strong, go-getter of a woman she'd grown to be took over easily. She reached out with her free hand and rested it on his cheek. She saw a flash in his eyes, and then his whole expression, not just his gaze, seemed to melt under her touch.

Ever so slowly, she began to lean forward and he met her halfway.

By the time his lips pressed against hers, the sun had met the sea at last, nature's glorious daily fusion beginning, bathing the two lovers in soft, golden light.

As the sea sighed and murmured by her naked feet, Spyri kissed her first love and her knees felt weak.

They pulled apart only for a second, just to exchange a glance of sheer bliss, then he squeezed her against him and his mouth sought hers again.

Spyri lost herself in his arms, her heart full, as he kissed her lips, her neck, her fragrant hair.

Chapter 8

Spyri and Markos crossed to the other side of the river mouth in one of the tiny boats. Markos handed a handsome tip to the local who took them across, jumped out onto the deck, and helped Spyri out by offering his hand.

She took it and teetered out of the boat, relieved to be on terra firma again.

"You certainly look a little green," he told her, seeing that when the boat rocked slightly as it moored earlier, her eyes had grown big like wagon wheels.

She retaliated with the speed of lightning. "At least, I didn't think I was crossing the Thames today!"

"Touché!" he exclaimed and took her hand in his. He kissed it, causing her heart to swell.

"Now, what? Where do you want to go, Mr Intrepid?" she teased.

He chuckled, then checked his watch. "It's seven. How about an early dinner? Get a cold drink while we wait for our order? I am parched."

"Ah! You said the magic word. A drink would be lovely. And dinner, of course. I'll even let you pick the place. Seeing you've been going without this paradise on earth for so long and all that."

His eyes ignited with excitement. "Ooh! Decisions decisions!" He rolled his eyes, scrunching up his face and looking all silly, then said, "Except, I know nothing about the establishments on offer. Perhaps we could stroll past a couple and decide together?"

"Sounds wonderful. On the beach or inland?"

"Surely, you don't need to ask me that. Beach, of course."

"Forgive me, what was I thinking?" she joked. They had now both fully regressed mentally back to that old summer of carefree, teenage foolishness.

"Lead the way, *Madame!*' he said, gesturing towards the lane that stretched out before them. The beach was a stone's throw away.

Holding hands, they walked to the shore, then took a wide boarded walkway along the seafront. It was lined with quaint tavernas and bars. The latter had colourful sofas laid out outside on the sand. Candles and lanterns were lit, the wicks trembling softly in the breeze.

"This is magical!" he said, meeting her gaze.

"It is…" she said, smiling sweetly, then turned away to offer a bitter, knowing smile to herself. She had walked along this beach many times over the years, looking at the young couples sitting on these seats at sunset. Such a romantic setting, and year after year her heart had been yearning to be there with him. *All these years I've waited… And now he is here… At last. But why? Why didn't he come back sooner? We could have had all these summers here… together…*

"Spyri? All okay?" she heard and spun her head around with a start.

She forced a nonchalant little smile. "Yes, why?"

"Oh! Nothing. You just seemed a little pensive, that's all."

"Look!' she said, pointing at the two tavernas they were approaching. The timing was perfect so they could change the subject. "These two restaurants, they are both exquisite. I highly recommend them, but, of course, you decide."

"Hm… They really look wonderful, I do admit."

He stopped short when they reached the space between them, and he led her closer to read the menus mounted outside both seating areas. "Oh!" he uttered when they'd had a look at both menus. "This one has Italian dishes as well as Greek ones. I quite like that. The other one is traditionally Greek, from the looks of things."

Spyri didn't care where they went. She was in heaven already. The feel of his warm hand wrapped around hers felt amazing. She raised her free hand and shook it before her face. "You decide. I am easy."

"What will you have if we choose this one then?" He pointed to the restaurant with the Italian choices.

"Perhaps a *bifteki*? Or the *moussaka*? They're both delicious here."

"So, you don't mind? I'm in the mood for pasta tonight. The more cheese the better." He smiled widely, eyes bright, like a child whose mother has promised to cook his favourite meal.

"Of course! You should have your pasta." Spyri couldn't help but giggle.

He tilted his head, brows raised. "What? What did I say?"

"Oh, nothing. I'm just happy to be here… with you…"

"Same here…" he said under his breath, capturing her gaze. Then, raising their joined hands, he kissed her fingertips.

Spyri bit her bottom lip, and willed her racing heartbeat to slow down. *Honestly. He has to stop doing that. Be still my heart…*

He gazed deeply into her eyes for another beat, then said, "Shall we?" Letting go of her hand, he gestured towards the seating area so she could step up to it first.

Moments later, they were sitting at a side table on the slightly elevated terrace with a generous view to the shore. The ambiance was perfect. The sea frothed at the sand below with a delicious little murmur, lanterns were lit all around, and a large wind chime at the corner of the thatched canopy tinkled at the soft breeze.

A seasoned waiter came to take their order and soon returned to bring a carafe of red wine and two glasses.

Markos poured the wine and chuckled when he met her eyes. "Thank you for not calling me boring when I ordered. I just had to have Spaghetti Bolognese."

"Why would I call you boring?"

"My pals back home do every time I order it. It's my favourite meal. My aunt Alexandra used to make it for me that summer. It's been my favourite meal ever since. Though it never tastes the same… It's never like my auntie's Bolognese.

Actually, I am hoping this restaurant will make it the same way, since it's in Corfu."

"That's strange! It's a simple recipe really... Unless she used a secret ingredient, perhaps?"

"Yes, I think that's it. Here in Corfu they have this special spice mix... I recall my aunt saying she always used it, but I can't remember the name of it. My mother didn't know either when I asked."

"Oh, that's a pity. But maybe we can ask the waiter when he returns."

"Let's wait first to see if the meal tastes the same!"

"Of course, let's hope it does!" Spyri said, crossing her fingers and giggling.

"You look so excited!" he said with a snorting laugh as he leaned back in his chair, an irresistible smile on his lips.

"And why shouldn't I be? If the meal has the same spice, it means you will recapture a memory from your childhood. That's always special..."

"That's true..."

"I know how that feels, Markos. Thanks to my grandparents, I have absolute loads of memories I can recapture any time I want. And it's always special. Tastes, smells, songs... tiny corners in the house, knickknacks, old cups and towels, cutlery... They all evoke memories. Actually, I think every crack in the pavement in my grandparents' front yard has the power to do that these days."

"I know... I mean, I wasn't lucky like that. I bet it's a wonderful thing to have that in your life. The house itself must be, for you, like a refuge you can always return to."

Despite herself, Spyri leaned forward and, instinctively, he did too. "Yes... That's exactly how it feels."

He took her hand in his and caressed her fingertips. "Oh, Spyri... How I wish this had been the case for me too. I wish we hadn't lost all these summers together."

Spyri felt at a loss for a few moments. She ached to know why he never returned but felt now she didn't have to ask him. His face had turned sombre, his lips closed tight as he seemed to try to find the words. So, she waited. The feeling of his fingers caressing hers felt amazing.

"You know... It wasn't up to me, Spyri. Ever since my only summer in Moraitika when we were kids, I spent every other daydreaming about it. Dreaming of you as well... missing you..."

"So, why didn't you come back?" she asked, despite herself.

"My mother wouldn't let me come back."

"What?" was all Spyri could utter in response. She knew it hadn't been his aunt's decision because all these years all she expressed was her wish for him to visit again.

"When winter came that year, my mother had a fight with both her sisters living here in Corfu, you see. It was about money matters... and something about the way their parents had split the land in Corfu among the two older sisters, leaving my mother in Salonica without a share, for reasons still unknown to me. And because of the row between my mother and her sisters, I was not allowed to return to the village again."

"Oh, Markos! I am so sorry..."

He shrugged his shoulders, his gaze dropping to his hands that were cupping hers now, and continued, "By the time I was old enough to pick my own holiday destinations, I was in love with a co-student, the woman I later married." He gave a forlorn sigh and added, "And now, this has ended with much heartache and a terrible betrayal on my wife's part. The moment I got out of that toxic relationship, my thoughts inevitably turned to my first love..."

He raised his gaze and pinned it on her, his lips breaking into a bright smile. "You! *You* are my first love, *Spyridoula mou!*"

Spyri felt herself light up, then start to melt like a candle on Holy Saturday mass. All she could do was smile back and will herself not to burst into tears. He used to call her Spyridoula that summer, on and off. It was her proper Christian name.

She had her grandfather's name, Spyridon – the patron saint of Corfu. For the sake of convenience, everyone had always called her Spyri, except for Markos. She found this so sweet. Especially now, as he had just used 'mou' with her name, the Greek word for 'my', in the endearing way the Greeks called their loved ones.

The waiter returned before she could say anything, but their eyes said all that had been left unsaid, their faces beaming with joy as the waiter set on the table dishes of mouth-watering food. Feta cheese tucked in phyllo pastry drizzled with honey and sesame seeds, tomato patties with herbs, *choriatiki* salad, fries, moussaka served with lashings of tomato sauce and cheese on top and, of course, Pasta Bolognese. The latter caused Markos's eyes to light up with sweet anticipation when it was set before him, causing Spyri to giggle anew.

"Well? What are we waiting for? Let's tuck in!" said Markos with a glint in his eye, holding up his fork like a trophy. "*Kali orexi!*"

Chapter 9

That night, Spyri lay down in Granny's old double bed. For the past hour, Spyri had been telling her all about her evening out with Markos.

"Say, Granny... Is there a special spice mix people use in Corfu? Markos was a little disappointed tonight. His Bolognese didn't taste the way he remembered it from his aunt."

"That's because Alexandra used *Spitseriko*. I've always used it too. Have you forgotten?" her grandmother's voice echoed in the semi-darkness.

"Oh yes... *Spitseriko*! Of course, I remember now. You used it in that pasta meal with the beef, yes? What was it called? Ah, yes! *Pastitsatha!* You did, didn't you, Granny?"

"That's right. Every pasta meal with tomato sauce is great with *Spitseriko*. It's wonderful in the *Pastichio*, too."

Spyri gave a deep sigh. "Pity the restaurant doesn't use it. Poor Markos... He looked so deflated after taking that first bite!"

"Not all restaurants are traditional, that's why. And it's not the kind of thing many of them will stock anyway. Small family tavernas maybe... It's not like you can get *Spitseriko* at the supermarket."

"Can't I? Where can I get it, Granny? I'd love to get some and cook Bolognese for Markos one day!"

"Oh, you should, *Spyri mou*! I can just see his face now. It'll be like he's eating at his aunt's table again!"

"That's the idea, Granny. But where do I get it?"

"There's only one place in Corfu town that prepares it, *Spyri mou*. It's an old pharmacy on San Rocco square. The address is in my telephone book downstairs. You know where it is. You can check it out tomorrow. Look under P. It starts with Pi... or something. Oh! My memory doesn't serve me well. But don't worry, you'll find it..."

"Thanks, Granny. That's wonderful!"

It was getting late now, but Spyri couldn't sleep. Sweet, enthralling memories from her perfect evening out with Markos kept parading before her eyes. Her heart was bursting, mind still whirling, and she knew it would be difficult tonight to surrender to sleep.

As she lay awake and looked out the open window, admiring the August full moon that hung high on the clear night sky, her grandmother's voice pierced through the darkness from beside her anew to make her chuckle. A feeling of warmth bloomed in her chest. Her grandmother's words had stirred an old, fond memory.

Whenever the August full moon was out, her grandmother would always make the same joke, asking Spyri if she fancied a stroll down the hill for a late night swim. Back in the 80s they used to actually do that but, of course, the passage of time had burdened her grandmother's body with terrible ailments. At her old age, the suggestion had been reduced to a precious old jest between them.

"Oh, Granny! You're so predictable!" said Spyri with a giggle. "How did I know you were going to ask me that tonight?"

Her grandmother laughed, then coaxed some more, carrying on with the joke. "I'll get the beach bag and the towels, you get the snorkel masks and the flippers."

"Oh, Granny! I love you so much!"

"I love you too, *kyra mou*."

"So, tell me, Granny... If you had a choice tonight between swimming in the sea and walking up the mountain to see the view of the bay, which one would you choose?"

"Ahhh... With dreams, you should never compromise, *agape mou*! Let's do both tonight!"

Spyri laughed bitterly, knowing her grandmother was forever a giggling young girl inside her heart, and wished she'd be like that too one day, as an old lady.

A few moments ensued in silence, and Spyri's mind drifted back to Markos. After their meal, on their way back to

Moraitika, they'd stood at the edge of the shore in a passionate embrace. Water was splashing on their toes, making them giggle. He'd taken her hand to kiss it and said, "I love you, *Spyridoula mou*. I always have..."

Spyri had gazed deeply into the green pastures of his eyes and melted, knowing then she'd found her childhood love again, and that this time she could keep him forever.

Her heart bloomed with warmth as she recalled his sweet kisses on their way back to the village. He had left her at the end of her lane with one last tender kiss, then waited until she'd turned the corner into her front door. The look in his eyes as he watched her go told her so much...

She put a gentle hand over her chest, a deep sigh escaping from her lips.

"All this sighing will cause us to miss our swim, you know! What about those flippers? Are we going or what?" piped up her grandmother, her voice echoing full of gaiety and teen-like cheekiness. Yet, it filled Spyri's heart with longing for the old days again, when all that was still possible, when even her grandfather was still strong enough on his legs to traipse up and down the hill with them for a swim.

"Oh, Granny..." A single tear rolled down Spyri's cheek as she looked up to caress the full moon with her eyes, feeling grateful for old memories and family love, the kind of love that had always served her as a compass. No matter how tough life would get this was the only place where she knew how to fix herself, how to pick up her life's pieces and to start anew.

It was as if she'd known her whole life. And it was no surprise that romantic love and the happiness that came with loving and being loved had found her there at last.

Chapter 10

The next few days till it was time for Spyri to return to England had passed quickly. It'd been a blur of utter bliss and joy for her and Markos. The only exception was the sadness of Mrs Alexandra's funeral. In the days that followed, Spyri helped Markos clear up his aunt's house.

They were considering putting it up for rent in order to stay for the long run at Spyri's house, but hadn't actually made a decision yet.

Markos was going back to Salonica soon but would return to the island in September, this time to settle down with Spyri there, for good. In the meantime, Spyri was going to try to sell her apartment and restaurant in London. In September, she would come to Corfu on a one way ticket, and would open a restaurant in the village as soon as she found the perfect opportunity.

As for Markos's work, he had a couple of websites where he marketed and sold various products, and this meant he could do business from anywhere in the world. Moraitika would work for them both just fine.

On the day of her departure, Spyri woke up next to Markos as usual, but, for the first time, instead of a smile, she had tears on her face. As soon as he stirred, she mumbled a good morning and offered to make breakfast, jumping out of bed.

It was early still and, as always, it was chilly. She found a cardigan thrown on a chair and put it on over her pyjamas, then hurried downstairs before Markos could see her tear-streaked face.

He came into the kitchen a couple of minutes later, rubbing one eye, his hair dishevelled. His voice was hoarse when he greeted her with a peck on the lips, and he froze when he caught a glimpse of her profile as she served tea in the cups.

Using an index finger, he lifted her chin to look at her better. "*Spyridoula mou*? You're crying? Why?" he said, dropping the jar of sugar he held carelessly on the counter to hold her by the shoulders.

Spyri gave a heavy sigh, avoiding his eyes. "Oh Markos... How can you ask why? Don't you know? This is our last day together..."

He chuckled and dried her tears with his fingertips, then kissed her tenderly on the forehead. "What nonsense is this? 'Our last day'? Honestly! While I draw air in my lungs, and for as long as you want me, we will be together, you know that! This is only temporary, *Spyridoula mou*! Come here, you silly girl..." He drew her into his arms and, for a few moments, she felt herself go limp. Her mind relaxed, and she drew in a luxurious breath as she smelled traces of his cologne on his polo shirt.

She sniffled and pulled away a few moments later, eying him like a scolded child. "I can't believe I'm flying back this morning. How am I going to leave you behind? I don't want to!" she piped up, sounding in her own ears like a wayward teen. She knew he was aching as much as she did inside, but, of course, he was the voice of reason for them both. He always had the right words to make her feel better.

Once again, he did just that, as he held her in his arms and caressed her hair. "Don't worry, *Spyridoula mou*. Now that we've found each other again, there's no one in the whole wide world that could tear us apart. And distance certainly cannot do that either. We both have sound proof of that, don't we?"

~~~

After a quick breakfast, they exited the house and walked up to the tiny village square where Markos had parked his car. He put her suitcase in the trunk and moved to open the passenger door for her to enter, but she placed her hand over his, her eyes pleading when she said, "A small favour, *agape mou*. Can we please pay a short visit somewhere before we get to the airport? It will only take a moment."

~~~

Markos drove them to the village cemetery, which stood on a small hill just off the main road that ran through Moraitika. The small cluster of tombs stood near a little chapel that overlooked the bay. The deep blue of the sea and the lush green fields were breath-taking. Still, there was no time to stand and admire the beauty today, unlike any other time when Spyri had visited this place.

Sure-footed, for she knew where she was going, Spyri strolled through the mossy graves. Most of them were crowned with big marble crosses.

She stopped in front of a grave, the two names that had been etched on the marble cross half-visible, blackened with humidity and the passage of time. One of the names was more visible than the other.

"Granny, Grandad, goodbye. I'm leaving today. But, as always, I promise to be back again soon. And this time, for good! I finally found happiness, the way you always wanted me to, Granny, remember?"

Markos placed a warm hand on Spyri's shoulder and squeezed gently. Her voice had started to falter, her feeling of sadness intense over the sudden death of her grandmother a few months earlier, but Markos's touch gave her new strength.

"Remember what you asked me, Granny, last summer? The last time I saw you? You asked me to bring you a man this year... you said you didn't expect to live much longer. I am so sorry you missed him, but here he is. I brought him here today for you to see. It's Markos, remember him? We love each other, and I am so happy! But I miss you so much... And I am so grateful to you for leaving me your house in your will, but you know what? It's simply impossible to be in your house and not see you, not hear you... You're everywhere, Granny. You're everywhere. Please, please, don't ever leave..."

By now, tears were streaming down Spyri's face, her voice breaking. Markos took her in his arms and she sobbed, and after a while, he gently reminded her it was time to go.

As they walked back to the car, Spyri turned around one last time to look towards the grave. "Goodbye Granny, goodbye Grandad. See you again soon."

Chapter 11

Spyri awoke in the middle of the night with a start. Her mind still rattled from the loud banging she had just heard. It had interrupted her peaceful sleep and now she felt disoriented. At first, she thought she was still in her apartment in London, but moments later she realized she was back in her grandmother's house in Corfu. She had arrived the previous day to start her new life there with Markos, as planned. She had sold her restaurant business, and all her belongings had been auctioned. All, except for what she could fit in the four jam-packed suitcases she had brought to Corfu with her.

Another bang echoed from downstairs. Just one, this time, or perhaps it had been something else. She had been sleeping soundly earlier, surrendered to a sweet dream about Markos, her one true love. He was scheduled to arrive in the morning, around midday, so they could start their joint life together, at last. *This can't be Markos. But who else could it be? No local would visit me at this unholy hour...*

She checked the old analogue clock on the bedside table. *Three in the morning... Definitely not a local paying a visit. But what if this is an emergency? A neighbour in need of assistance?*

That caused her to jump out of bed and turn on the lamp on the bedside table. She stood and grabbed her phone, walking barefoot on tiptoe. Only once she began to descend via the internal staircase did it occur to her that this might be a robber, and not someone in need. This filled her with dread, and she decided against turning on any lights downstairs. Just in case the electric light would be visible from the outside through the window shutters. She preferred to remain stealthy if she were to near the door and listen intently for any signs of a presence on the other side.

Reaching the ground floor, she suffered a moment of paranoia. It led her to open the cutlery drawer on her grandmother's decrepit kitchen cabinet. She peered inside, using her phone to see in the darkness. When her gaze rested on the kitchen knives, she shook her head with dread. *That is not me. No way.* The alternative was one of her granny's discoloured wooden ladles. Another shake of the head. *Please.* Taking a step towards the door, she remembered her grandfather's ornate cane that still stood in the corner by the door. Her grandmother had never had the heart to give it away, and nor did she.

That'll do, if need be... Pity Grandad never used a baseball bat in all his life. She allowed herself to chuckle inaudibly at the ridiculous thought, despite her trepidation. There was no sound coming from the door, and this, by now, had led her to believe that there was no one there, after all.

She caressed the handle of her grandfather's cane with her fingertips, more for moral support at that point, rather than for any other reason, careful to keep it steady in its place. Then, she stood before the door and pricked her ears. All she could hear was the owls tooting away in the trees.

"Who's there?" she asked under her breath, just in case.
Nothing.

"Could it be it was just a dream?" she mumbled to herself. Then, feeling very confused, for she could have sworn she'd heard that loud banging for sure, she went back upstairs. Relieved, and allowing herself to dismiss the whole thing, she climbed into bed and didn't give this strange incident another thought.

~~~

"Markos! My love!" she exclaimed, standing at the edge of the tiny village square when his car parked before her. He had driven up the narrow winding road that led there from the bottom of the hill. She and Markos had spoken on the phone earlier when he reached Lefkimmi's humble little port on the ferry.

She knew that within half an hour he would be home. Yet, too restless to stay indoors, she had spent the last fifteen minutes at the square, sitting on a ledge in the shade of a mulberry tree, her phone keeping her company so the time could pass more easily.

"*Spyridoula mou!* At last!" he said when he got out of the car and drew her into his embrace. Nestled against his chest, wrapped in his arms, she felt like a wounded little bird that had finally found both shelter and healing.

Their passionate kiss, their firm embrace, and the tender look in his eyes when they pulled apart told Spyri in an instant all she needed to know. He loved her, and he had no qualms about this at all. Like her, he had arrived at Moraitika to spend a whole life together with her. Never looking back to their previous lives again, to all those years they'd spent apart. From now on, they had a new life to lead. A joint life of bliss in the place that had brought them together so many years ago. By now, she didn't even lament the lost time any more.

A lot of soul-searching in the past months had led her to believe that everything happens for a reason. Perhaps, if they hadn't both had these separate lives, they wouldn't be the same people they were today – the people who had found each other after twenty years and clicked together immediately, effortlessly, like two jigsaw pieces that had been made for that very same purpose.

Giggling, she asked to see his suitcases in the trunk, and he, chortling, led her to the back of the car to oblige her, his arm around her shoulders. They had been joking back and forth for days, each betting they would be the one to bring to Corfu fewer things from their old lives. He was confident he would win the bet, "seeing that he was a man". As he'd put it, "Women tend to carry all sorts of useless things anyway."

He had said all that in jest, of course, and she had mock-scolded him in return. She was also confident she'd win, though, since he was subscribing to a bunch of magazines (about fitness and fishing, apparently) and had sounded unwilling to part with his old stock.

Now, opening the trunk, he caused her to see that the bet was a tough one to win, after all. He had packed four suitcases too, roughly the same size as hers. When she revealed to him this fact, he laughed out loud.

"I think we may have to settle for the fact that there is no winner here," he put to her.

"It's not over until the measuring tape has spoken! We have to measure the cubic meters of the luggage. No other way to determine this," she retorted and he kissed her forehead, laughing out loud.

"We'll get these later," he said when he sobered, closing the trunk. "Let's go home, *agape mou*. I am starving!" he said, taking her hand in his. "Is there anything for lunch?"

"Are you joking? Of course, there is. Your favourite. I've made Bolognese."

His eyes opened wide. "With *Spitseriko*?"

She cocked her eye at him. "Is there any other way to make it?"

He gave a woot and squeezed her hand in his with fervour. Picking up speed as they headed home hand in hand, he was almost dragging her along now.

"What is it with you men and your food?" she said, giggling, as she hurried alongside him.

"Oh come on, Spyri! Stop laughing! I'm starving, I tell you! That tepid cheese pastry I bought on the boat to eat first thing in the morning settled in my stomach like a brick."

~~~

The two had enjoyed their pasta with a green salad, fresh *choriatiko* bread, and local Corfiot olives. The latter had been an offering from Spyri's Great-aunt Fotoula, her grandmother's only surviving sibling, who lived in the neighbouring village of Spileo. Her grandson, Stergios, had left them at the house the previous evening as a welcome gift after Spyri called her aunt to let her know she'd arrived on the island.

Over the years, her aunt had never stopped providing Spyri's grandparents with offerings of olives and cold-pressed extra virgin olive oil. Her grandchildren were tending the family olive groves and fields these days.

"Oh my! How lucky am I to have fallen for a chef?" said Markos when Spyri returned from the kitchen with a platter of the *chalva* she'd made that morning. She used a mixture of thick and thin semolina in equal measure to get the texture just right, as per her grandmother's old recipe. These days, people enriched the traditional dessert recipe with cooking chocolate, bastardizing it, but she refused to do it. Besides, it was too sickly sweet on her palate that way.

Markos loved it with a generous sprinkling of cinnamon powder and so did she. To please him, she had omitted the chopped almonds inside as this was how he preferred it.

Once they had enjoyed their dessert, she invited him to settle on the sofa and rest in front of the TV while she cleaned up the table and did the dishes.

He put up a firm hand. "No way. You know I could never do that. We're partners in all things, remember? We split everything fifty-fifty. Including the chores. You clean up and I do the dishes? Or the other way around. Either way, I'm good."

She beamed at him and he gave her a peck on the lips, the light in his eyes like a radiant sun warming her all the way down to her toes. She offered a sweet smile. "Okay, *Partner*. You clean up here and come find me. I'll be in the kitchen working up a lather."

Moments later, they were standing side by side in the tiny old kitchen, their elbows rubbing together, causing them to giggle. "I am glad I like you. As, if I didn't, this close proximity would be quite a problem," he joked.

"I am glad you *like* me!" she said, emphasizing the word for fun, and he tittered like a mischievous school kid. She was rinsing plates and cutlery, and he was in the process of drying the glasses and the pans with a tattered kitchen towel.

"So? Have we decided? Are we going to stay here? Not my aunt's?"

She whipped her head around to gaze into his eyes. "Yes, that's what we decided, didn't we? But... Why do you ask? Have you changed your mind? You can tell me if you have. You can tell me anything, Markos. You know that."

Chapter 12

Markos shook his head profusely, then put up a hand and caressed her cheek. "I know, *Spyridoula mou*... Absolutely no secrets between us. Ever..." He gave a soft sigh. "To be honest, I only asked because I have something on my mind that's making me wonder..."

"Why? What is it?" asked Spyri, concerned when she saw a shadow cross his face.

He scoffed as he rubbed his chin. "You promise you won't laugh if I tell you?"

"No, of course not. What's troubling you?"

He must have guessed she felt alarmed because he put up both hands to cradle her face, then said with a smile: "No, no, no! It's nothing serious, *Spyridoula mou*, trust me! It's only about this silly dream I had last night."

Spyri felt her earlier panic lift from within her, like a clutch of feathers caught in the wind. She wasn't sure what had caused her such deep concern. The idea he might have cold feet, perhaps. Inwardly, she admonished herself for her lack of faith. In him. In them. "What about the dream?" she said a moment later, seeing he continued to look at her, lips pressed together.

"It was a dream about my aunt Alexandra," he revealed finally. "About her, and this very house. I took it as a sign. A sign that we're supposed to live here, in your grandmother's place, since you love it so much. And to rent my aunt Alexandra's, as opposed to doing things the other way around.'

Spyri let out a soft sigh. "Thank you, Markos... I do appreciate you are still happy to do that. For me... But... I don't understand. What makes you think the dream was a sign? What did you see?" asked Spyri, who had always believed in signs. With her eyes wide open, she had forever sought them throughout her life for guidance. Even when her eyes were shut, she looked with the eyes of her soul in her dreams, to find them.

They had both just finished with their respective chores so he led her back to the living room, promising to tell her there. They sat on the sofa and he said, "In my dream, my aunt was standing outside, banging at this very door." He pointed to the front door that was shut at the time. "And I was standing outside with her, just watching her. She didn't acknowledge me, just kept banging at the door, non-stop."

"What? I don't believe it..." Spyri mumbled to herself. Hearing the word "banging" had led her to make an instant connection to her peculiar incident the previous night. All the details returned to her mind vividly.

Unaware, Markos carried on, "She was holding two shopping bags. They were made of clear plastic, containing things. Food, I think, of some sort..."

"And she was banging at the door, you said?"

"Yes. Like, really loudly!"

"And then? What happened?"

He must have registered her bright expression then, because he put a hand on her shoulder, squeezing it gently. "*Spyridoula mou*? What is it? Why do you ask me like that?"

So she told him what had happened in the middle of the night.

Aghast, he gazed into her face for a few moments. His eyes focused far, though, and she could tell he was trying to decipher his dream again, this time in connection with her own nightly experience. A few moments passed in silence, then he added, "I don't know what to make of this, *agape mou*. And I haven't even told you the rest of my dream yet. It got weird next."

"Like, how?"

"Well, at some point, your grandmother answered the door. When she did, both she and my aunt disappeared. By the time the door was fully opened, both had been replaced, if I can call it that, by two beautiful young girls..."

"Girls? What girls? Do we know them?"

"No, I can't say that... They looked similar, like twins... Both tall and thin, with flowing brown hair that had blue ribbons on them. They had honey-coloured brown eyes that were warm with kindness. With love... They looked like angels... I could almost see a shimmer around their heads. They looked like halos." He scratched his head, lips pressed together, then added, "Yes, I guess I can say with certainty that they looked angelic."

Spyri nestled closer to him and he raised an arm to hold her against him. Getting comfy against the crook of his arm, she let out an inaudible sigh and said, "Surely, that's a good dream... And perhaps the two angels may be a sign that you and I are meant to live here?" she said, still dumbfounded by the odd way his dream tied with her rude interruption last night. *Or, maybe, that was a dream too...*

"Perhaps..." he replied. "So... What about *your* experience last night? What if the banging noise wasn't real? What if no one was really there, and this was, in fact, a dream with a message from my aunt Alexandra? To you?"

Spyri pressed her lips together and shook her head. "I don't know. I could swear the banging was real. But there was no one there when I went downstairs. So, yeah... Perhaps it was a dream, after all. A very vivid one at that."

Markos squeezed her against him and kissed the top of her head. He opened his mouth to speak, but then, a voice echoed from behind the closed front door.

"Hey! Anyone there? Spyri, you in?"

Like in all other old homes in this village, there was no doorbell on this front door either. The locals tended to shout out for the door to be answered.

Spyri smiled to her ears. She had recognised the voice immediately. She patted Markos's hand. "It's my Aunt Fotoula! Let's see if you remember her from that old summer!" Excited, they both jumped to their feet, and she swung the door open.

Aunt Fotoula stood there dressed in an elegant green top, black skirt, and sandals. Her face was deeply wrinkled, yet bright with her joy to see Spyri again. Her eyes emitted a strong light, despite her old age, the kind that only a heart full of love can muster.

Spyri gave her a warm hug, then introduced her to Markos.

Aunt Fotoula patted his hand and chuckled. "I remember you, Markos! When Spyri told me about you, I pictured you effortlessly on my mind from that summer when you came to stay with your aunt. You had such a kind face, and you still do. You've turned into a fine man. Spyri is lucky to have you. But, I hope you don't mind me saying, you are even luckier to have *her*!"

Markos laughed and nodded profusely. "Oh, don't I know it!"

"*Ela, Thia*! Come, Aunt! Come inside and sit!" said Spyri, beckoning for her to enter. As her aunt moved gingerly to the sofa, Spyri added: "But, how did you get to Moraitika? You're not on your own, surely!"

Aunt Fotoula laughed as she took a seat. "Of course not! These frail old legs can hardly carry me to the bathroom these days," she joked. "Stergios brought me. He has an errand to run, then he'll come and get me."

Spyri excused herself and returned a few moments later from the kitchen, bringing a glass of fruit juice and a plate of *chalva*. "I made the dessert myself, Auntie. I hope you like it."

"Oh, thank you, *Spyri mou*. I love *chalva*. But I'll have only a little piece, just to try it, as I haven't had lunch yet, and I'd hate to spoil my appetite." She smiled amicably and took a bite. "*Ya sta heria sou, koritsi mou*! Health to your hands, my girl!" she said, using the Greek figure of speech to thank a cook for a job well done. "I really can't tell this apart from your granny's *chalva*." She raised her glass and drank to Spyri and Markos's good health, and they wished her the same.

Once she'd had a few sips, she continued, "Ah... that was much needed, thank you. It's so hot out there today. I don't normally leave the house at lunchtime, but today I'm going all the way to Benitses! Two friends of mine are on holiday there, you see... They're from Ioannina. We haven't seen each other in years. When they invited me for lunch I didn't know what to do, but Stergios offered to drive me there, bless him."

"Oh, that's nice!" said Spyri and Markos in unison.

Aunt Fotoula's eyes went ablaze, then she continued, "He takes such good care of me! You know, he'll leave me in Benitses to have lunch with my old friends, then drive all the way back to pick me up again. He's a gem, and I know I'm lucky to have him!"

"Yes, indeed you are, Aunt Fotoula," replied Markos.

"And you? When did you arrive to Corfu?" she asked him.

"A couple of hours earlier," he said, his face bright.

"And you are both here to stay this time?"

"Yes!" they said together, Markos reaching out to take Spyri's hand in his.

Aunt Fotoula beamed at them. "I'm so happy for you both! But where will you live now? This house?" She shifted her gaze from her niece to Markos, her expression benign. "Or your Aunt Alexandra's?"

Chapter 13

It had been a casual question, but, somehow, it had caused Spyri a tug in her insides. Markos pressed his lips together and looked at her mutely, and that was all the confirmation she needed to know this was still a thorny subject. All he'd told her was he was happy to leave the decision up to her. But what did he really prefer? That, she didn't know.

She turned to her aunt and managed a faint smile. "We are not fully sure yet, but, most probably, we are going to live here, Auntie. In my grandmother's house. She wanted me to live in it once she was gone, and I feel her presence in every nook and every corner..."

"I know, my darling... I feel her too, now that I'm here." She looked around, then gave a deep sigh. "Goodness knows, I feel my late husband's presence in my old home too. I could never leave it for that reason."

"I'm glad you said that, Auntie. It goes to show I am not crazy thinking like that. I only hope Aunt Alexandra won't mind us putting up her home for rent, if she's watching us from Heaven."

"Of course, she won't mind... Alexandra would never oppose anything that would make your grandmother happy, believe me," assured them both Aunt Fotoula, her gentle gaze shifting from face to face like a little bird skipping playfully from branch to branch.

"*Spyri mou*, your grandmother and Alexandra... they were like sisters. They had always been so close. Not surprised they died with one year's difference either. They were sister souls, if you ask me..."

"I didn't know they were so close..." said Markos, leaning forward in his seat.

"Yes... I was only a small child when they were young girls, but I remember them vividly. They were forever walking up and down the lanes together, holding hands. We smaller kids in the village used to call them, 'The Twins', you know?"

"The Twins?" said Spyri and Markos in unison. Their faces must have been alive with surprise because Aunt Fotoula chuckled loudly.

"Yes. But why do you find it so strange?"

Spyri and Markos exchanged one knowing look, then Markos said, "Oh, just taken aback, I guess... Were they the same age, then?"

"A couple of years difference, tops, I should think..."

"Did they look alike, Auntie?" asked Spyri, trying to conceal her growing mystification.

"Yes, as a matter of fact, they did. That's mainly why we called them 'The Twins'. Not just because they were inseparable. I remember once, especially, they turned up at a wedding, both dressed in white dresses, blue ribbons on their wavy long hair..."

At the mention of the blue ribbons, Spyri whipped her head around to check Markos's reaction. He looked like the wind had just been knocked out of him. He gave her a mute glance that telegraphed, even more palpably, that he was awestruck. Inwardly, Spyri told herself all this striking detail in his dream couldn't possibly be a matter of coincidence.

Unaware of their inner mystification, Aunt Fotoula rattled on, "Those two looked almost identical! Oftentimes, it was like you were seeing double! They wore similar clothes and colours all the time. From a distance, you could never tell them apart." She gave a hearty laugh, but Spyri hardly listened to her by then. She was too busy telegraphing her sense of wonder back and forth with Markos as their gazes remained locked together.

"You could see them together in that old picture, if you like! See for yourselves..." Spyri heard her aunt say a few moments later, and it snapped her back to the present.

"What picture, Aunt?" she asked, her heart skipping a beat.

Aunt Fotoula gave a vague wave towards the old kitchen cabinet. "It's in there. You know where your grandmother kept her old black and white photos, don't you? That old tin

My Corfu Love Story

box? I bet you it's still in there. The picture from that wedding."

Spyri stood like a spring and opened the double cabinet doors. Sure enough, the tin box lay in the exact same corner at the bottom shelf where it had always been. She'd taken it out countless times since her childhood to browse through old photos and hear her grandmother's stories.

She returned to the sofa and, placing the box on her lap, removed the lid slowly, with reverence. With tender hands, she picked up a few photographs, caressing them with her fingertips. It struck her then that this was the first time she opened the box since her grandmother died.

A lump formed in her throat, and when Markos offered to take a few photos from the box and help her look, she obliged him with a simple nod of the head.

It didn't take long to find the photograph of that age-old wedding. Spyri found it and showed it to her aunt for confirmation, then handed it to Markos while she continued to scrutinize it with her eyes. Now she saw it again she remembered it from before. She even recalled her grandmother pointing out where she was in it, but, somehow, she didn't recall her naming Mrs Alexandra as one of the other people photographed around the bride and groom.

But now, thanks to Aunt Fotoula, who had just confirmed, she knew who Alexandra was among all the youngsters. She stood beside her grandmother in the photo. All the small children and some of the adults, even the bride, were looking timidly at the camera. But the two teenage girls stood tall and confident before the photographer.

Indeed, they looked very similar, their beautiful faces radiant, their long dresses reaching down to just under their knees. A basic cut, but so elegant.

Their hair flowed generously around their shoulders, ribbons adorning woven strands on both sides of their heads. Although this was a black and white photograph, she knew the ribbons were blue. Thanks to Aunt Fotoula... And Markos's dream, of course.

The two old friends had visited them both last night in unison, to tell them they were all right. And perhaps to also tell them that this house was where Spyri belonged with Markos, after all.

"See what I mean? Like twins!" said Aunt Fotoula, bending forward to tap at the photo gently with one gnarled finger.

Spyri nodded, still lost for words, while Markos's stumped expression told her, without a shadow of a doubt, that these were the twin girls he'd seen in his dream.

A voice echoed from the door, which, this time, they'd left open to allow the cool breeze to come in. Stergios stood there, two plastic bags in hand.

Two clear plastic bags. With food, no doubt... The moment Spyri saw them she couldn't help but stare for a while, gobsmacked. Was there an end to the clues these two angels had given them both last night? Tying them all together provided perfect clarity of their message by now.

"*Yassas*! Hello!" Spyri's cousin exclaimed with a wide smile. "*Ela, Yaya!* Come on, Grandmother! Let's go! You're going to be late for your appointment in Benitses."

Aunt Fotoula gave a kindly smile. "*Ne, efcharisto*, Stergios! Yes, thank you!" They all stood and joined him at the door.

Aunt Fotoula took the bags from his hands. "We brought these for you from our land," she said, handing them to Markos.

Spyri kissed her cousin on both cheeks and introduced him to Markos, then they both expressed their thanks. The bags were full of fresh organic produce. Such a generous and precious gift! Tomatoes, cucumbers, aubergines, peppers, and even some okra. The latter was just enough for one plate perhaps, but they could share. Some of the tomatoes were dark red and soft to the touch. They practically begged to be used in a tomato sauce. The okra meal would be fantastic with freshly grated tomato. With some fries, bread and feta cheese, they would make for a hearty lunch for two.

Aunt Fotoula kissed them both goodbye and left with Stergios without further ado.

Closing the door, Spyri turned to Markos and cocked her eye at him. "Your aunt carried two bags in your dream, you said?"

He chuckled loudly. "I think we've just deciphered my dream to the full." He gave a lopsided grin, leaving the bags on the table. Turning to her, he opened his arms wide to let her in.

Revelling in his warm embrace, Spyri raised her head and lost herself in his eyes. "Don't forget my dream too... It was your auntie banging at the door. Now, I know it!"

"Same time I had the dream too, no doubt!" He shook his head with disbelief. "That's a point. What time did you have your dream? I know I had mine around three a.m. because I woke up shortly after and had a glass of water. I checked the time on my clock."

Never leaving his tender gaze, she smiled. "You guessed it. Three a.m."

He put up a hand and caressed her cheek. "I have to say, I am amazed... and relieved too. To know we have their blessing to live here. To be honest, I had been feeling guilty for planning to put up my aunt's house for rent."

Spyri felt relief wash over her like a jet of tepid water, soothing her to the core. Finally, she identified the thorn pricking their insides all along. Guilt. His and hers. But their angels had just removed all that from their lives.

She smiled widely at him, and he mirrored her expression, his eyes dancing. "Well, Markos... now we know your aunt doesn't mind if we live here. She came with my granny last night to give us her blessing. They both did."

"Wow. Just wow..." it sufficed him to say before he kissed her tenderly on the lips.

When they pulled back, Spyri let out a soft sigh, leaning her head on his chest. Markos kissed the top of her head, cooing at her, as if she were a baby, and she felt safe, loved, and perfectly in place. They had all the time in the world to make this a fully functional, comfortable home to house their life together. Her grandmother's old house was going to make for the perfect love nest to last them a lifetime.

Already, she was making plans to extend the building towards their small garden on the back. Just enough for one extra bedroom… She wanted kids. They both did. And they also had plans to start a business together.

Already, she was getting excited about finding the perfect taverna to purchase. She could already see it in her mind's eye. She would take care of the cooking, and he would work his magic with the marketing, each using their professional experience of the past. They'd make a killer team. Both as business partners and as parents…

But, for now, all she wanted was to start a life with him. A life where everything revolved around the two of them. For the foreseeable future, she was going to dedicate every waking moment to getting to know him, to strengthening their bond, and to making new, loving and fun memories with him, every day. Making him the centre of all she had worth living.

His voice brought her blissfully back to the present. "Ah, *Spyridoula mou*… It's a comfort, isn't it, to discover that our deceased loved ones never truly leave us… To know that your granny and my aunt are both still here. Guiding us… Telling us that we have their blessing to live in this house together."

"And so we shall," she said, as she met his eyes that burned like twinkling stars. "And so we shall, my darling…"

THE END

Keep turning the pages for FREE books from this author!

My Corfu Love Story

Did you know? Every time one of my readers forgets to write a review, a Corfiot gets so upset that they forget to pick the olives from their trees. It just breaks my heart! Tell me what you thought of this book and help the Corfiots continue to pour olive oil in their salads!

Please leave a short review on Amazon. It will be greatly appreciated!

Direct link: http://mybook.to/Corfulovestory

A NOTE FROM THE AUTHOR

This book wouldn't have been made possible without the continuous support and encouragement of my husband, Andy, and the assistance of my always eager beta readers. I thank you all, and especially Louise Mullarkey for taking the time to polish the manuscript to a shine with her usual tender loving care.

I originally published this romance with the title "A Holiday with Granny" in my short story collection, "Facets of Love". The copy you've just read is an extended version.

It was inspired by my deep love for my late grandmother, Antigoni Vassilakis, and the village of Moraitika.

If you'd like to see pictures of the places described in this book, you're welcome to visit my humble travel guide to Moraitika and Messonghi: http://effrosyniwrites.com/your-guide-to-moraitika-corfu/

Both these villages are perfect for families and quiet couples. I recommend them highly for your next beach holiday. But I have to be honest – once you go there, you'll want to go back every year. So be warned, LOL!

Did my references to the traditional Greek dessert of *chalva* make you curious about it? Here is my family recipe: http://bit.ly/1IjeeDY. It's one of my favourites. Give it a go and enjoy!

MORE FROM EFFROSYNI

In my bimonthly newsletter I share FREE kindle book offers in every issue and fun news from my life in Greece. You'll get two ebooks instantly as welcome gifts when you join!

Go here to sign up:
http://effrosyniwrites.com/yours-for-free/

Award-winning, new adult romance set in Moraitika, Corfu. Inspired by the author's summers there in the 80s with her grandparents. A standalone read, yet, the paranormal twist at the end creates a strong premise for the rest of the series.
Visit Amazon http://myBook.to/pierseries

Beach fun, magic spells and unrelenting suspense. The last twist will blow your mind! Available in 4 kindle episodes or a boxset.
Visit Amazon: http://mybook.to/ravenboxset

A paranormal romantic comedy that tugs at the heartstrings. Kelly ran a marathon and wound up running a house. But the ghost wasn't part of the bargain! This delightful read features a playful ghost and a quirky pug: http://mybook.to/RunHaunted

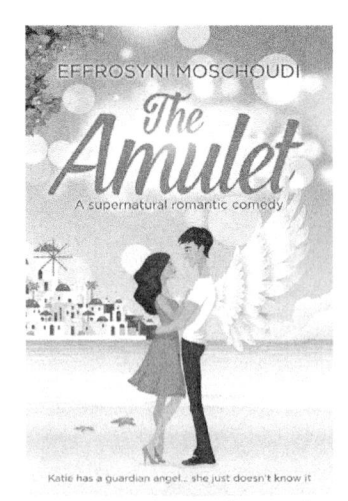

A paranormal romantic comedy with quirky characters that will entertain you no end! Set in a small family hotel on the island of Sifnos. Katie has no idea she's fallen for her guardian angel and the mysteries pile up, driving her crazy! http://myBook.to/Amulet

ABOUT THE AUTHOR

Effrosyni Moschoudi was born and raised in Athens, Greece. As a child, she loved to sit alone in her garden scribbling rhymes about flowers, butterflies and ants. Today, she writes books for the romantic at heart. She lives in a quaint seaside town near Athens with a British husband, two naughty cats, and a staggering amount of books and DVDs. Her little town is heavenly enough, yet her mind forever drifts to her beloved island of Corfu.

The Ebb, her new adult romance that was inspired from her summers in Moraitika, Corfu in the 1980s, is an ABNA Q-Finalist. Her debut novel, The Necklace of Goddess Athena, won a silver medal in the 2017 book awards of Readers' Favorite. Her ghost romance novella, The Boy on the Bridge, was a Top 10 winner in the "50 Best Indie Books" awards of Readfree.ly in 2021.

Effrosyni's novels are Amazon bestsellers, having hit #1 several times, and are available in kindle and paperback format.

Go here to grab FREE books from this author: http://effrosyniwrites.com/free-stuff/

Visit Effrosyni's website for free excerpts, book trailers, her travel guide to Corfu, and a plethora of blog posts about her life in Greece: http://effrosyniwrites.com

In this blog, she shares her favorite Greek meals with the world. Visit at your own peril - it will make you feel ravenous! https://effrosinimoss.wordpress.com/category/greek-recipes-2/

Effrosyni is always delighted to hear from readers and highly values any comments!

**Email her at ladyofthepier@gmail.com

**Friend her on Facebook:
https://www.facebook.com/efrosini.moschoudi

**Like her page on Facebook:
https://www.facebook.com/authoreffrosyni

**Follow her on Twitter: https://twitter.com/frostiemoss

**Find her on Goodreads:
https://www.goodreads.com/author/show/7362780.Effrosyni_Moschoudi

Printed in Great Britain
by Amazon